EDGE BOOKS™

SPIES

SPY
[SKILLS]

by MICHAEL MARTIN

Consultant:
Jan Goldman, EdD
Founding Board Member
International Intelligence Ethics Association
Washington, D.C.

Capstone
press®

Mankato, Minnesota

Edge Books are published by Capstone Press
151 Good Counsel Drive, P.O. Box 669, Mankato, Minnesota 56002
www.capstonepress.com

Library of Congress Cataloging-in-Publication Data
Martin, Michael, 1948–
    Spy skills / by Michael Martin.
    p. cm. — (Edge books. Spies)
    Summary: "Discusses the skills and abilities needed for the field of
espionage"— Provided by publisher.
    Includes bibliographical references and index.
    ISBN-13: 978-1-4296-1308-8 (hardcover)
    ISBN-10: 1-4296-1308-4 (hardcover)
    1. Espionage — Juvenile literature. 2. Spies — Juvenile literature. I. Title.
II. Series.
UB270.5.M3654 2008
327.12 — dc22   2007033577

Editorial Credits
Angie Kaelberer, editor; Bob Lentz, designer; Jo Miller, photo researcher

Photo Credits
Alamy/Arclight, 8; Arthur Turner, 18; Greg Brown, 7; Iain Masterton, 9 (left);
    Rodolfo Arpia, 14; Simon Belcher, 29
AP Images, 27 (both); RTR-Russian Television Channel, 21
Corbis/Bettmann, 17; Jeffery L. Rotman, 9 (right); Roger Ressmeyer, 10
    (background)
fotolia/Andrea Seeman, cover
Getty Images Inc./AFP/Luke Frazza, 25; Photonica/Beverly Brown, 13;
    Taxi/Shiva Twin, 4
Shutterstock/Aga, 6; Andy Piatt, 3; Black Ink Designers, Corp., 4, 30;
    Dejan Lazarevic, 6; Feng Yu, 5; John Wollwerth, 1; Perov Stanislav, 17
SuperStock, Inc./age fotostock, 22
ZUMA Press/Chris Kleponis, 10 (foreground)

1 2 3 4 5 6 13 12 11 10 09 08

TABLE of CONTENTS

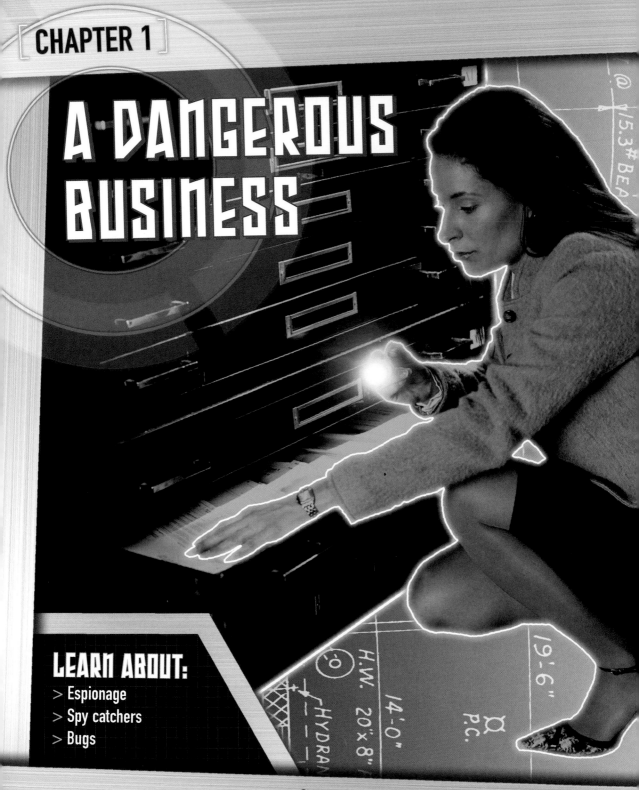

CHAPTER 1

A DANGEROUS BUSINESS

LEARN ABOUT:
> Espionage
> Spy catchers
> Bugs

> Some spies examine top-secret files for valuable information.

Have you ever spied on someone? Maybe you secretly followed your friend at the mall. Or perhaps you listened on an extension phone when your sister talked to her best friend. Spies do similar things, but they do them as part of their jobs.

A spy's mission is to gather valuable information without being noticed. Collecting information secretly is called espionage. The information collected is called intelligence.

Spies collect intelligence in different ways. They may break into an office where top-secret documents are kept. They copy or memorize the documents. Other spies take secret photos of another country's new weapons or military vehicles.

intelligence

sensitive information collected or analyzed by spies

A SECRET JOB

The best spies do their jobs without anyone noticing what they are doing. They are experts at blending into society. They have to be. Their lives may depend on it.

Successful spies are intelligent and quick-witted. They must sometimes talk themselves out of tight spots. They also have to gain the trust of people who have information they want.

SPY FACT

Captured spies sometimes agree to become double agents. To avoid prison or death, they agree to give false information to their employers.

> Spies always try not to be noticed by others.

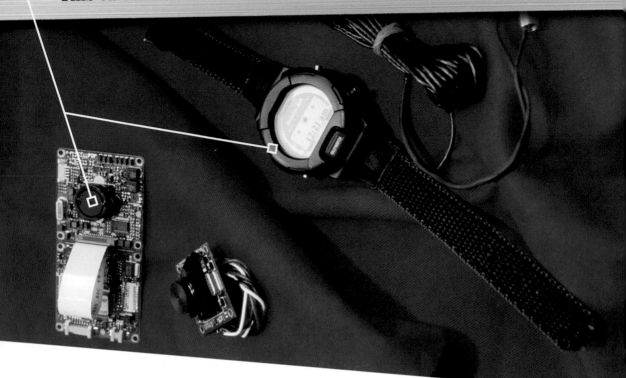

A wristwatch holds a tiny video camera (right).
This camera sends its information to a receiver (left).

A BAG OF TRICKS

Spies use tools to help them collect intelligence. Some spies carry tiny hidden cameras that fit in wristwatches, belt buckles, or even shirt buttons.

Other spies hide tiny listening devices called bugs in places where secrets might be discussed. Bugs transmit conversations to recording devices or listening posts. At these places, people can listen to the conversations without being noticed.

A bug can be hidden almost anywhere. It could be placed inside a lamp or a clock. Or it might be hidden in a book, pen, or painting.

Spies are always looking for new ways to collect information safely. Devices like bugs and hidden cameras are useful. But the best intelligence often comes from other people. The trick is getting them to provide it.

Video cameras that fit in the palm of the hand are useful spy tools.

The East German spy agency Stasi used this camera hidden behind a button.

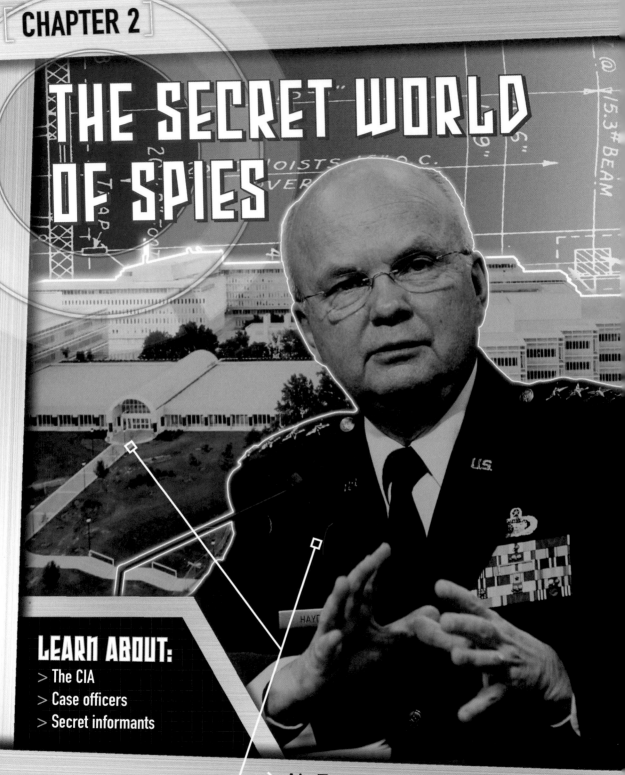

CHAPTER 2

THE SECRET WORLD OF SPIES

LEARN ABOUT:
> The CIA
> Case officers
> Secret informants

Air Force General Michael Hayden became director of the CIA in 2006.

Most countries have agencies where professional spies work. The Central Intelligence Agency (CIA) collects intelligence in foreign countries for the U.S. government. The United Kingdom has two intelligence agencies. MI5 collects intelligence inside the United Kingdom. MI6 collects information in foreign countries.

The KGB once spied for the Soviet Union. In 1991, that country split up into Russia and several smaller countries. The Federal Security Service (FSB) now collects intelligence for Russia.

Spy agencies do more than just collect information. An important part of spying is protecting government secrets from other countries. This work is called counterintelligence. In the United States, a part of the Federal Bureau of Investigation (FBI) handles most counterintelligence duties.

---

counterintelligence

the actions of an intelligence agency designed to protect secret information from enemies

SURVEILLANCE

Spies always assume someone is on their trail. A spy walking on a street might quickly change direction to see if anyone follows. If so, the spy may be under surveillance.

How do spies escape being followed? They might suddenly jump onto a bus or subway car. Or they might enter a store and then quickly slip out a side door. They also could quickly change their appearance by putting on or removing a hat or sunglasses.

surveillance

the act of keeping very close watch on someone, someplace, or something

SPY FACT

Counterintelligence agents are very careful during surveillance. They work in teams and switch off every few hours or even minutes.

> Spies do their best to avoid surveillance.

> Informants can be one of the best sources
of intelligence.

NETWORKS AND INFORMANTS

Agents sent to another country often become part of a spy network. A case officer supervises a network. Spies usually know little about their case officer or other spies in the network. The spy agency keeps the spies apart on purpose. Captured spies are questioned and even tortured for information. The less spies know about others, the fewer people they can put in danger.

Before going on dangerous missions, spies look for easier ways to collect information. Sometimes the best way to get information is to talk to people who already know the secrets. These people are called informants.

informant

a person who provides information

RECRUITING

Case officers who recruit informants look for people who have the knowledge they want. The officers might try to make friends with foreign military or government officials at a club or a party.

Once a friendship has begun, the case officer looks for the person's weaknesses. Perhaps the person needs extra money or is unhappy with his or her job. When the time is right, the case officer will ask for secret information. If the person provides it, he or she is caught in the web of spying.

LOOKING FOR A FEW GOOD SPIES

Case officers also recruit new spies. They look for experts or people who have access to important people or locations. Computer experts might be good recruits. They could easily learn how a government stores its information.

SPY FILES: INVISIBLE INKS AND SECRET MESSAGES

Spies must communicate without being discovered by the enemy. Sometimes they use secret codes or write messages using invisible ink. The message can be read by putting it under a special light or by adding a special chemical. Another way to disguise secret writing is to print a photo on top of it. Later, a chemical applied to the picture will remove the photo and reveal the message.

Scientists also can be good recruits.
They often work on projects that aren't
known to the general public.

CHAPTER 3

GOING UNDERCOVER

DRIVING LICENCE

UK

UK
PASSPORT SERVICE

An Executive Agency of the Home Office

Reference Number: 56

Mr Andrew Carr

Spy agencies create false documents for their agents.

Spies entering an enemy country risk their lives. They need all the help they can get to survive. A good false identity, called a **cover**, is the strongest protection of all. A spy with a false identity is undercover.

PRETEND PEOPLE

Spy agencies spend a lot of time and energy creating false identities. Undercover spies need to be good actors with good memories. They memorize a made-up life history of the person they are pretending to be.

Spy agencies are also experts at forgery. They create passports, birth certificates, and other documents that support the cover story. These fake documents look just like the real thing. But they won't fool anyone unless the spy memorizes the information. Imagine forgetting the birthday assigned to your new identity!

cover

a story used to disguise a spy's true identity, motive, or actions

SENDING INFORMATION

Once spies collect information, their job is only half done. They must get that information safely and secretly to those who can use it. Spies may need to learn secret codes or how to use a hidden radio transmitter.

One way spies pass information is through dead drops. A dead drop is like a secret post office for spies. It is a prearranged location where messages, money, or secret equipment can be left for pickup.

A dead drop location might be a hole in a tree trunk. It could be a tiny container on the underside of a park bench or beneath a bridge. One spy even used a hollowed-out wooden cross in a cemetery to pass his messages!

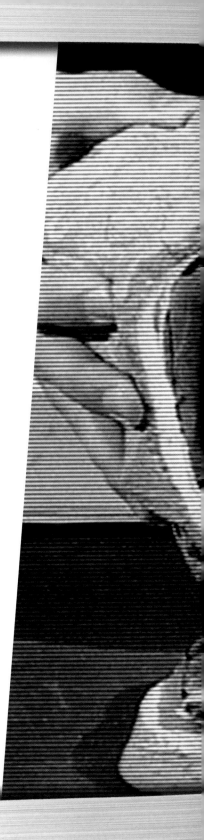

To most people, this dead drop looked like an ordinary rock. Spies placed information in its hollow center.

CHAPTER 4

MOLES, DOUBLE AGENTS, AND SLEEPERS

LEARN ABOUT:
> Spies deceiving spies
> Aldrich Ames
> Sleeper agents

> Double agents can do deadly damage
to the country they are working against.

Good spies must be able to judge whether someone is lying. For example, a new recruit may not be a recruit at all. He or she might be a **double agent**.

Double agents try to get recruited by a spy agency. But they already secretly work for an enemy agency. Once they're hired, they pass along the intelligence they collect to the enemy agency. They also give false information to the agency that employs them.

MOLES

The most damaging double agents are called moles. Moles work inside a spy agency for years. At some point, they become loyal to another country. Because they are trusted agents, moles often rise to positions of power. Most moles are also very careful. They are almost never seen doing something suspicious.

double agent

a spy who works for one country's spy agency but is really loyal to another

A FAMOUS MOLE

In the 1980s, the CIA thought Aldrich Ames was one of its most trusted agents. Ames had worked for the agency since 1962. By 1985, he led the CIA division that worked against the Soviet Union's KGB.

But the CIA didn't know that Ames couldn't pay his bills. To pay off his large debts, Ames started selling CIA secrets to the KGB in 1985. Over the next several years, the KGB paid Ames more than $2.7 million. The KGB also kept another $2 million for him in a bank.

Ames' CIA job allowed him to share valuable secrets with the Soviets. His information caused the deaths of at least 10 KGB double agents working for the CIA. In 1994, Ames was convicted and sentenced to life in prison without parole.

> In 1994, Ames was arrested, tried, and sent to prison for life.

SLEEPER CELLS

Moles like Ames are so difficult to catch because they may go years without doing anything suspicious. Sleeper agents are also difficult to catch. These spies enter another country. They live and work there in ways that seem completely normal.

SPY FILES: A FAMILY OF SPIES

John Walker was a U.S. Navy warrant officer who worked around secret codes. In 1967, he went to the Soviet embassy in Washington. He offered to provide information about those codes in exchange for money. The Soviets agreed. They set up a system where he could pick up his money at dead drops.

Over the next 18 years, Walker provided information that allowed the KGB to decode 1 million top-secret messages. Walker later recruited his brother and his son, who were also in the Navy, to spy with him. In 1985, Walker's ex-wife turned him in to the FBI. He was convicted and sentenced to life in prison.

Years and years can go by. Then, the sleeper agents receive a coded message. It might be left at a dead drop, delivered by mail, or transmitted by radio. At that moment, the agents become active spies.

> Walker as a Navy officer (left) and at his arrest in 1985 (right).

For example, sleeper agents might be ordered to gather intelligence on weapons factories in their new country. This intelligence could be used in terrorist attacks. But because sleeper agents have lived normal lives for so long, they are unlikely to be suspected.

The real mission of a spy is hidden until the very end. In the shadowy world of espionage, no one is ever quite who they seem to be.

SPY FILES:
INCREDIBLE SHRINKING PHOTOS

Spies use special cameras to take pictures of secret documents. The images they produce are called microdots. They are so small they can only be read by a microscope or a viewer that magnifies the image. Microdots are not much bigger than the period at the end of this sentence.

Spies can make microdots with a simple camera. First, they take a photo of a document. When the film is developed, they hold the film up to a lightbulb and take a photo of it. The receiver uses a magnifying glass to read the words in the microdot.

> An ordinary person on the street could be
a master of espionage.

GLOSSARY

counterintelligence (koun-tur-in-TEH-luh-gens) — the actions of an intelligence agency designed to protect secret information from enemies

cover (KUHV-ur) — a story used to disguise a spy's true identity, motive, or actions

double agent (DUH-buhl AY-juhnt) — a spy who works for one country's spy agency but is really loyal to another

espionage (ESS-pee-uh-nahzh) — the actions of a spy to gain sensitive national, political, or economic information

forgery (FORJ-ree) — the crime of making illegal copies of paintings, money, or other valuable objects

informant (in-FOR-muhnt) — a person who provides information

intelligence (in-TEH-luh-juhnss) — sensitive information collected or analyzed by spies

recruit (ri-KROOT) — to ask someone to join a company or organization

surveillance (suhr-VAY-luhnss) — the act of keeping very close watch on someone, someplace, or something

READ MORE

Stemple, Heidi E. Y. *Ready for Anything! Training Your Brain for Expert Espionage.* New York: Scholastic, 2006.

Stewart, James. *Spies and Traitors.* North Mankato, Minn.: Smart Apple Media, 2007.

Townsend, John. *Spies.* True Crime. Chicago: Raintree, 2005.

Walker, Kate, and Elaine Argaet. *So You Want to Be a Spy?* Spies and Spying. North Mankato, Minn.: Smart Apple Media, 2003.

INTERNET SITES

FactHound offers a safe, fun way to find Internet sites related to this book. All of the sites on FactHound have been researched by our staff.

Here's how:
1. Visit *www.facthound.com*
2. Choose your grade level.
3. Type in this special code **1429613084** for age-appropriate sites. You may also browse subjects by clicking on letters, or by clicking on pictures and words.
4. Click on the **Fetch It** button.

FactHound will fetch the best sites for you!

INDEX